Teddy Bear, Teddy Bear

A Traditional Rhyme

ILLUSTRATED BY

TIMOTHY BUSH

Greenwillow Books, *An Imprint of* HarperCollinsPublishers

Teddy Bear, Teddy Bear: A Traditional Rhyme
Illustrations copyright © 2005 by Timothy Bush
All rights reserved. Manufactured in China.
www.harperchildrens.com

Watercolors were used to prepare the full-color art.
The text type is Bodoni Classic.

Library of Congress Cataloging-in-Publication Data
Bush, Timothy.
Teddy bear, teddy bear / by Timothy Bush.
p. cm.
"Greenwillow Books."
Summary: An illustrated version of the traditional rhyme, which follows
the activities of a teddy bear who is lost and tries to make his way home.
ISBN 0-06-057835-1 (trade). ISBN 0-06-057836-X (lib bdg.)
1. Nursery rhymes. 2. Children's poetry. [1. Teddy bears—Poetry.
2. Nursery rhymes.] I. Title.
PZ8.3.B9755Te 2005 [E]—dc22 2004042402

First Edition 10 9 8 7 6 5 4 3 2 1

Greenwillow Books

For all the friends I've made along the way—T. B.

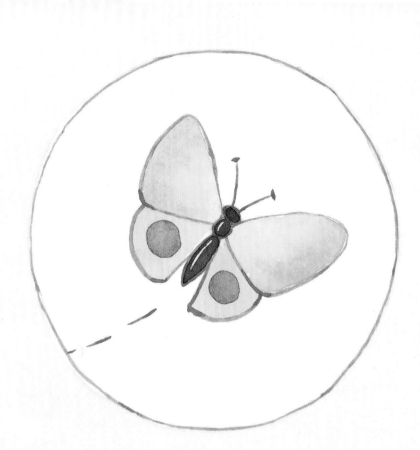

Teddy Bear,
Teddy Bear,

touch

the

ground.

Teddy Bear, Teddy Bear, turn around.

Teddy Bear, Teddy Bear, say hello.

FOUND!

Hello.

Teddy Bear,
Teddy Bear,

Teddy Bear, Teddy Bear,

jump

up

high.

Teddy Bear,
Teddy Bear,

touch the sky.

Teddy Bear, Teddy Bear,

whew!

Where's my bear?

go upstairs.

Teddy Bear, Teddy Bear, say your prayers.

Teddy Bear,
Teddy Bear,

turn out the light.

Teddy Bear,

Teddy Bear,

say **good night!**

Teddy Bear, Teddy Bear,

touch the ground   turn around   say hello   off you go   jump up high

touch the sky   go upstairs   say your prayers   turn out the light   say good night

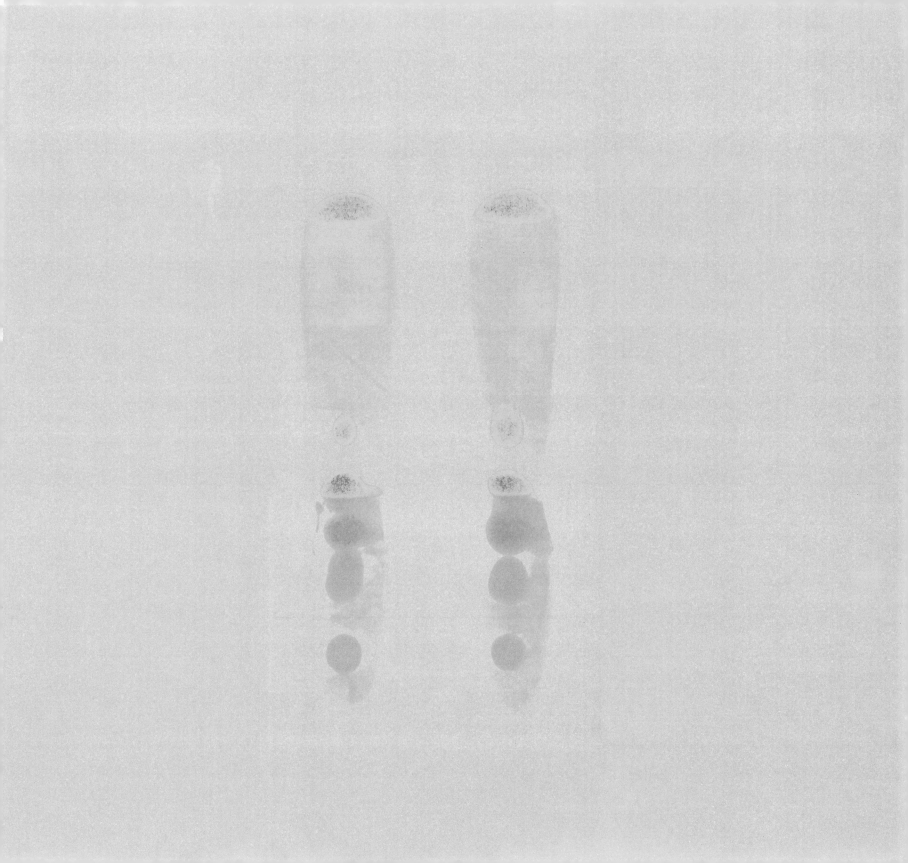